JANIE PLANTS A TREE

WRITTEN BY
RITA WELLS

ILLUSTRATED BY
G.W. EVERETT

WestBow
PRESS
A DIVISION OF THOMAS NELSON

THIS BOOK IS
DEDICATED TO
MY MOTHER
WHO MADE THIS ALL
POSSIBLE AND REMAINS THE
GREATEST INSPIRATION IN
MY LIFE.

A long time
ago
there was a
little girl
named
Janie...

One day at Janie's school, a local tree nursery was selling trees for a penny. Janie searched her pockets, found a penny, and bought a tree, so she could plant it herself in front of her house.

She skipped happily home that day with the tree in her hand, and she wished as hard as she could that she might grow as big as the tree...

But Janie didn't know that her little tree
was a Poplar tree that would grow very tall.
Janie's wish was about to come true.

Janie planted the little Poplar tree, and she watered and cared for it every day.
The tree began to grow, and kept growing...

and growing...

and growing...

and growing!

Janie grew in the same way. She grew and
grew so tall that her mother had to use a ladder
to reach her and give her some food.

Janie could no longer enter her house because she was so tall. She stood by the tree both day and night. She just watched as the other children played. This made her very sad and unhappy.

She spent most of the night crying. This made the Poplar tree very unhappy too. The tree loved Janie and only wanted to make her happy by granting her the wish she had made.

One night when the moon was big and bright and the stars were twinkling, the tree asked Janie why she was crying so, and Janie replied, "Oh! I am very unhappy because I am sooooo tall. I didn't know that you would grow so big and so tall, tree, and that my wish would really come true! I cannot go into my house any more, or play as the other children do."

...So the tree hung
its branches in sadness
and said, "I only
wanted to grant you
your wish, Janie.
You cared for me and
loved me so. But if
it will make you happy
once again, I will ask
the Fairy-Out-Of-The
Deep-Blue-Sky to help
you."
So the tree called,
"Fairy-Out-Of-The-Deep
Blue-Skies,
Come and dry Janie's eyes."

Suddenly the Fairy appeared, and she said:
"Oh, mighty Poplar tree, what is it that you ask of me?"
And the tree answered:
"My wish for Janie is that you would make her happy, if you could.
Please change Janie into her natural size once more, so that she can play like she did before.
And to live in her house and do what the other children do.
Is this too much to ask of you?"

Then the
Fairy-Out-Of-The-Deep-Blue-Sky
waved her magic wand and

ZAPPPPPPPPPPPPP!

There stood Janie
as pretty as a
picture.
The mighty Poplar
was towering
over her.

Early the next morning, Janie's mother came out with the ladder to feed her breakfast. She was so surprised to see this beautiful young girl standing beside the tree. Janie's mother walked up to the young girl and said...

"Could you please tell me where my Janie is?"

And Janie smiled and replied,

"Why, Mother, I AM Janie!"

"The Fairy-Out-Of-The-Deep-Blue-Sky
made my wish come true last night. She has
made me into my natural size again and now I
can come in the house, and live with you, and do
what other children do!"

Janie and her mother were so happy that they held hands and danced with joy around the Poplar tree.
The mighty Poplar tree was happy too, because he knew that he had made Janie very happy.

Each day Janie would sit under the mighty Poplar tree and think about the little tree she had bought with a penny and planted in her yard. A tree that had grown from a little twig to an amazing, towering tree. And Janie was thankful that she was a small and happy girl again.

THE
END

CPSIA information can be obtained
at www.ICGtesting.com
Printed in the USA
BVIC011100100413
317796BV00002B

* 9 7 8 1 4 4 9 7 8 9 0 3 9 *